AF425085

J.C. HULSEY BOOKS

# SHADRACK
## A WESTERN SHORT
## J.C. HULSEY

For information contact: jchulsey1@att.net
Cover Art by **Yusuf Idris**
Cover Design by J.C. Hulsey
Published by J.C. Hulsey Books
September 2020
10 9 8 7 6 5 4 3 2 1

# CHAPTER ONE

He was thin, tall and raw boned. His face looked as though it was chiseled from granite. His gunmetal gray eyes had a cold, calculating look about them. His chestnut brown hair was showing grey from under his brown sweat stained Stetson. He was riding a large Tennessee Walker with a blueish color. He sat tall in the saddle as if he were a part of it. Around his waist was a plain well-worn brown gun belt attached to a matching holster. The gun was a new Colt. 45 Peacemaker. The newest addition to the Colt firearm company. On closer look, the weapon was clean and still had a new look to it, unlike the holster which held it. As he rode down the middle of Main Street, he looked neither to the right nor to the left, only straight ahead like a man with a purpose. A man with but one thing on his mind.

The man's name is Shadrack Meshack. He's known in almost every town and settlement in the western territories as Shadrach the Avenger because just as the Biblical Shadrach was rescued by an angel of God from a blazing fiery furnace, so also had Shad Meshack escaped from the fire that destroyed his home and took the life of his sweet wife and baby girl. He has the scars to attest to the fact that he barely escaped with his life. It had been three long, lonely years since that fire had claimed his family.

"However long it takes," is what he told his friends, "however long it takes, I will find the men responsible and mete out justice of their choosing. Be it a hangman noose or a bullet from my gun. They will face their maker one way or another."

He rode straight to the sheriff's office as was a habit he had started a long time ago. He wanted the law to know why he was in their town in case he ran into the men he had been searching for all these many years. Most of the lawmen listened and agreed that they wouldn't interfere if he faced the accused, however, there were a few hard-cases that told him flat out if he drew his gun in their town, even in self-defense and someone was killed he would be locked up.

Shad listened calmly, then stood up to his full height of six feet seven inches, looked the lawman in the eye with those cold, calculating eyes and said, slowly and clearly so there would be no misunderstanding. "Sheriff," he said so quiet the sheriff had to strain to hear. "You don't want to get between me and what I have to do either before or after. I've never killed a lawman. I would hate for you to be my first."

Most of those so called hard-cases were just a lot of hot air. They looked into Shad's eyes and started back peddling. "I'm sorry, Mr. Meshack, I was only trying to keep peace in my town like I was hired to do. Please, you carry on with what you have to do. I'll not interfere. I hope you find your adversaries real soon."

Shad tipped his hat, nodded to the man and left the building. He untied the reins and walked up the street to the livery stable. He stopped at the door, holding the reins in his left hand, leaving his right free to take care of business should the occasion arise.

"Howdy, stranger," said the hostler, a man, looked to be in his forties wearing dirty brown trousers and an even dirtier white shirt covered with a greasy leather apron. "I seen you ride in. Rode straight to the sheriff's office. You one of them bounty hunters or something?"

"How much to stable my horse?" Shad asked, ignoring what the man had said.

"Not much of a talker, are you?" the man asked.

"Is this a stable or a question and answer place?" asked Shad.

"Didn't mean nothing, just making small talk. Be a dollar a day for your horse unless you want extra grain? 'course if you leave him for a whole week, the grain comes free."

"How much for all week?"

"Five days or seven?" The hostler asked.

"I ain't got a whole lotta book learning," said Shad, "but the way I remember is a whole week, as you put it, is seven days."

"That'll be five dollars for seven days. How's that sound?"

"Don't make no difference how it sounds, if that's the price, then that's what I'll pay. Here's ten dollars. If I come back to get him and see you done a good job, it's all yours."

"Thank you kindly, Mr. . . . . I didn't catch your name."

"I didn't throw it, but it's Shad Meshack."

The hostler's face turned beet red. "I'm real sorry Mr. Meshack, if I spoke outta turn. I'm just an old coot sometimes lets his mouth overload his, well you know what I'm trying to say. Didn't mean nothing."

"No harm done. Just look after my horse, he's mighty special to me."

"Yes sir, I'll treat him like he's my very own. He'll get nothing but the best. That's a promise."

Shad nodded, satisfied his horse would be well taken of. He turned and walked out the door and headed for the local watering hole by the name of Singing Dove Saloon.

As he got closer, he heard a beautiful voice singing a song he used to hear his wife sing many years ago. He stopped at the swinging doors, peering over the top, scanning the room trying to locate the faces of the men that were burned into his brain the way the fire had scared him. The woman's voice seemed to stir up memories long forgotten, maybe not forgotten, but stored away in the deep recesses of his brain.

He pushed through the doors easing to the side scanning the room a second time. When his eyes reached the singer, he felt as if someone had punched him in the gut. The woman was a spitting image of his dead wife. Grabbing a chair, he eased his tired body into it. He sat staring as if mesmerized by this woman. As she sang her eyes were looking around the room to make each person think she was singing directly to them. When her eyes reached Shad, she missed a beat in the song, but quickly got back on track. However, her eyes stayed on his face. When the song was over, she walked directly to his table.

"You're him aren't you," she asked, her eyes still locked on his.

"Depends on who him is? Who you think I am?"

"Why you're Shad Meshack. You were married to my sister."

"Melissa never said she had a sister. I think she would have told me, as close as we were."

"We were separated when our parents divorced. I went with Papa and Lisa went with Mama."

"I have to admit the way you look threw me for a loop. You're the spitting image of Melissa."

"I heard what happened. I wanted to come then, but didn't have the money to make the trip. I wanted to send a telegram, but I couldn't even get enough money for that. By the time I did pull together enough, you were moving around so much, I didn't have a place to send one."

"How come you're working in a place like this? How come you ain't married?"

"I was married. Happily married for almost a full year, then he was killed when he went to the bank. It was that day that Carmelo Martinez and his gang decided to rob the bank. Charley didn't lay down on the floor quickly enough so they killed him."

"You said the Martinez gang was responsible?"

"Yes."

"They're the same bunch that burned our home, killing Melissa and Margie. I almost died, but didn't. I've spent the last three years searching for them."

"I've got to get back to work," she said, looking around. "If I don't sing, I don't get paid. Will you stay until I'm finished? I have a million questions for you."

"I'll stay," he said. "I've got a couple of things I want to ask you."

Shad sat there continually scanning the room, observing every man that entered.

*'Ain't that something, I didn't even ask her name. Well, plenty of time for that.'*

Her voice was sweet and smooth. As he sat listening, he could hear some of the same inflections in her voice as Melissa had. *'Her voice, combined with her looks, threw me for a loop. Here I am on a mission to track down the men responsible for the death of my wife and child. I don't have time nor inclination for any detours, yet something about this young woman grabbed my attention and hung on. It shouldn't hurt to detour for a short time to learn more about my new found sister in law.'* Shad sat, listened and watched her closely. *'I got to admit she must be who she says she is, because she's so much like my wife in so many ways.'* As he sat there, he scanned the room again, but still didn't recognize anybody.

It was getting late and he was anxious to move on yet that voice kept calling for him to stay, so he stayed.

He checked his watch. It was a little after midnight when she stopped singing and walked to his table. She said, "Come on, let's get out of here. If I stay, somebody will want to visit."

"Where we going?" asked Shad.

"I've got a room in the hotel. Ain't much, but it's all I can afford."

Shad followed behind her noticing the way her hips swayed from side to side.

"Let's go up the back stairs," she said as she turned down the alley beside the hotel. "Bentley, the desk clerk wants to talk every time he sees me."

"Sounds like you're a very popular woman."

"I've been singing in that place going on four years, and yes, you might say Marissa Nelson is well known and most of the men are always hitting on me."

"Did you ever think about grabbing one of them and settling down?"

"I thought about it on more than one occasion, but I couldn't find the right man. This is my room." She turned the door knob and stepped inside. "Come on in."

Shad stepped through the door, brushing her as he passed. It was a small room. A bed, a dresser and a small armoire in the corner.

Marissa noticed him looking around. "I told you it wasn't much. Sit on the bed and close your eyes while I get outta my working clothes, if you don't mind."

"How about I step outside while you do that?" He turned and went out the door pulling it closed.

In a few minutes, he heard, "Okay, you can come on back."

He went back inside and sat on the bed. Marissa looked a little different without . . . as she put it, her working clothes.

Shad could notice even more familiar things about her that reminded him of his wife.

She sat next to him and began, "Our parents named us Melissa and Marissa. Mama and Papa were mismatched from the very first. Why or how they ever got together in the first place has always been a mystery to me. Papa was a rugged outdoorsman and Mama was a high society woman. She stayed with him as long as she could and then decided she couldn't take anymore. Melissa and I had just turned ten. I didn't understand then and I still don't understand how they decided who would go with whom. My sister and I were not only sisters, but we were buddies, friends, confidants, if you will. I think it hurt more being separated from her than it did losing my mama. I cried constantly for a week. I never heard from Mama or Melissa again until I was almost eighteen. By then Papa had died and I was alone and on my own. What can a newly turned eighteen-year-old girl do to get by? You're looking at it. Thank God I was blessed with a singing voice so I didn't have to sell my body. I could have made a lot more money by doing that, but somehow it just didn't set right in my mind.

"You said you were married," said Shad.

"Yes, I had been singing for about six months when I met Charley. There was something different about him. He wasn't like the rest of the men who kept pestering me. We got to talking and I began to have feelings for him. When he asked me to marry him, I said yes. Then, he was killed in that bank robbery I told you about."

"So you went back to singing in the saloon?"

"There wasn't anything else I could do. I always planned on saving enough money to try and find my sister, but I make barely enough to get by. Then three years ago, I heard about a man who had survived a horrific fire that killed his wife and child. It was a big story, making the front page of the paper here. That's all that was talked about for weeks all over the country. The story told the names of the victims. One of those names was Melissa along with your name, of course, and a young child. How did I know it was my Melissa, you may ask? I can't explain how I knew. When I saw that name on that newspaper page, I felt as if a piece of my heart had been ripped from my body. I knew then, at that moment, the next place I would see my sister would be in Paradise. I wanted so badly to attend the funeral, but again, I make just enough to barely get by.

"Your husband didn't leave anything for you. Like money, anything?"

"No, he owed more than he had. The little place we had was repossessed by the bank almost before Charley's body was in the ground. I've been watching and waiting for the day that you would come through those doors. I heard of the quest you're on to find the men that did this and mete out the justice they deserve.

Singing in a place like this and having to mingle afterwards, I hear a lot of things. About six months ago I overheard some men talking about something that happened some years back. They were bragging, you might say, about torching a man's home. It seemed like a big joke to them. They were laughing about the way the woman and kid screamed as the flames engulfed the building. But they said what was even funnier than that was when the man ran from the fiery inferno, his body covered with flames. They said he looked like a walking torch with arms failing to and fro. They rode away, leaving the burning house and the walking torch, laughing and patting one another on the back telling how they had done such a good job. Maybe they would collect a bonus."

"You said one of them was a Mexican? Big fat and ugly? Kind of don't care attitude?" he asked.

"Yeah, that was one of them. He didn't say much. I don't think I ever saw him crack a smile," she explained. "Are they the ones?"

"Could be. You see which way they went?"

"I did," she said. "Because of what they said, I wanted to know where they were headed."

"Which way?" Shad asked a little irritated.

"I'll tell you on one condition," she leaned close looking intently at him.

"What condition?" he asked.

"Take me with you," she stated emphatically.

"You crazy?" he spat the words out, starting to stand.

"Wait, Shad. Hear me out at least," she pleaded.

He eased back onto the bed, looking at her with a quizzical look.

"First and foremost, I'm Melissa's sister. I have a right to see these lowlifes six feet under," she continued, "I can handle a gun as well as any man and I can hit what I shoot at."

"I'm a loner. I don't travel with nobody, let alone a woman."

"All I ask is give me a chance to prove to you I can take care of myself. If you don't agree, then we'll part company."

"I'm going against my better judgement, but meet me at the east edge of town at six in the morning and show me what you got." He stood and walked out of her room.

# CHAPTER TWO

The next morning after a breakfast of eggs, flapjacks and coffee, Shad walked to the edge of town.

Marissa was there dressed in men's trousers and shirt, which only accentuated her full figure. On her hips were twin Colt 45s, which looked to be well worn on the grips, from lots of use.

Shad stood a moment, taking in the sight with a surprised look on his face.

"Well," he said strolling toward her, "you are dressed the part, but clothes don't mean nothing when you're facing down a killer. Come on, let's go a little further away from this metropolis."

They walked about five hundred yards further and Shad stopped, drew his weapon and fired at a small tree in the distance, breaking off the lowest branch.

He hadn't gotten his gun back in the holster when two more branches were broken off by Marissa's twin guns.

"I'm impressed, but what would you do if someone did this?" he twirled and grabbed both guns from her hands.

"I'd do this," he felt the sharp edge of a knife against his throat.

"Okay," he said. "That's good up close. How about far away with the blade?"

She removed the knife from his throat and in one fluid movement the knife was thrown into the large tree some feet away.

Shad stood staring as if hypnotized by what he had witnessed.

Marissa took her pistols from his hands, discarded the spent cartridges and replaced them.

She slid them easily into the holsters and asked, "Convinced?"

"I have to agree you can handle a gun and knife, but that don't make you my partner. Have you ever shot a man?"

"No. Have you?" she asked with a little too much confidence.

"I've killed a few, but we're not talking about me, now are we?"

"Shad, you know I have as much right to hunt down Melissa's killers as you? Please, I promise I won't be no trouble."

"You got a horse?" he asked.

"No. I had to save a lot of money to get these guns."

"If I agree and I say if. . . you do everything I tell you without question. And just so's you know, we ain't going after'em to kill'em. We're gonna bring'em back to stand trial. Is that understood?"

"Understood," she said eagerly. "When we gonna head out?"

"Just as soon as we get you a horse and buy supplies. I figure sometime this afternoon. Provided we can get a decent horse in this sorry town."

"Hey, you're talking about my home. Well, it's been my home for some time now."

"Come on, let's go to the livery stable." He took off at a brisk pace. Marissa had to scurry to keep up.

They arrived at the livery stable and walked inside.

The hostler was busy brushing an animal and didn't see them at first. He walked around the horse and spotted them.

"Oh, hello there Mr. Meshack, didn't see you come in," he said nervously. "You gonna be wantin' your horse?"

"No. I'm. . . well me and the young lady here are looking to buy a horse. You got anything worthwhile?"

"No, Sir. I don't have nothing here that I'd want to sell to you, Mr. Meshack, "however I can tell you where to go. There's a horse ranch about four hours west from here. The Rocking R. Best horses in three counties. You tell'em Moody sent you. They'll treat you square."

"Okay, Moody, was it? You got something the young lady can ride out to this horse ranch?

"Yes sir, I do, I'll be right back," he turned and went out the back door, only to return almost immediately. He was leading the sorriest broken down nag Shad had ever seen.

"This here's Mildred, she don't look like much, but she's reliable. You want I should throw a saddle on her for you?"

"You bring out my horse while I saddle her." He began the ritual of saddling the mare. Something that he could do with his eyes closed.
He was finishing up when Moody came in with Shad's horse saddled and raring to go.

"Here you are, Mr. Meshack. When you get where you're going and get another horse, just turn Mildred toward town and swat her on the butt. She'll come back on her own. I also filled your canteens for you."

Shad nodded to Moody, glanced at Marissa who was already in the saddle. "Let's ride," he said and left at a gallop.

They rode the four hours in silence. Shad kept stealing glances at Marissa, shaking his head and asking himself what he had gotten into.

They rode through a gate with a sign proclaiming *ROCKING R RANCH - HORSES BOUGHT AND SOLD.*

Shad slowed his horse to a walk; Marissa did the same.

"You let me do the talking," he told her.

"I believe I can do my own bargaining for a horse. I'm quite capable of handling things myself."

"If this is the way you're gonna listen to me and do what I say, then we may as well turn around and go back to town," he told her. "But, just for your information, most cowpoke don't want to deal with someone of the opposite sex. And besides that, there is one other reason."

"Yeah, what's the other reason?"

"You ain't got no money."

"Yes sir, I hear and obey," she held up her hands in mock surrender.

They rode into the yard of a large adobe house with a larger barn out in front.

A man dressed in dungarees and a blue chambray shirt stepped away from the corral where a horse was being worked.

He removed his hat, wiped the interior with a bandana, placed it back on his head and looked up just as Shad and Marissa stopped in front of him.

"Can I help you folks? I'm Randy Rogers. I'm the foreman here."

"We're looking to buy a horse for the young lady here," said Shad, scanning the area as he always did.

"Step down and let's see what we got for you," he turned before they dismounted expecting them to follow.

Shad climbed down and indicated Marissa do the same.

"Remember, let me do the talking."

Marissa didn't answer, just took off in the direction following the foreman.

"I believe we have just what you need right over here, he guided them to a small corral. "There she is," he pointed to a small Appaloosa mare.

"I don't think she's what we're looking for," Shad told him.

"Don't be so hasty in your decision," said Rogers. "You may not be familiar with this breed. The Nes Pierce Indians in the Northwest Territories breed them for stamina. If I was a betting man, I'd bet this little more would outlast your horse," he hesitated. "I tell you what, why don't you take her for say, one week. If she's not everything I said, then you bring her back. How's that sound?"

"How much you asking?" asked Shad, watching Marissa, who was fully infatuated with the mare.

"How much you willing to pay?" asked Rogers.

"Come on, Marissa," Shad said abruptly.

"But, Shad?" she whined.

"I said come on," he turned to leave.

"Hold on, partner," said Rogers. "Did I say something wrong?"

Shad turned back and faced the man. His steel gray eyes looking daggers at him. "I figure a man should put a price on something and not dicker about it. We came here because we were told you would treat us fairly. Now, if you want to sell the mare, give me a price."

"I can see now I ain't dealing with no greenhorn. I'm asking an even 100-dollar bill for the mare and that includes a saddle especially made for her."

Marissa turned her eyes and looked directly into Shad's eyes. There was a mournful puppy dog look in her eyes that Shad couldn't say no to. "Alright, we'll take her." He reached down deep into his pants pocket and pulled out a well-worn leather purse. He opened the drawstring and pulled out a wad of bills. He unrolled it and counted out five twenty-dollar bills, handed them to Rogers and closed the purse placing it back in his pocket.

Marissa grabbed Shad and gave him a big hug. His arms involuntarily went around her and it felt as if she belonged there.

"Dobe!" called Rogers. "Bring the mare and Brant, you git the small saddle from the tack room." The men took off in opposite directions.

The young man named Dobe led the horse to where we were standing just as Brant came walking up with the saddle. "You want I should saddle her, Boss?" asked Brant.

"I want to saddle my new horse," exclaimed Marissa.

"Yes Ma'am," both the drovers said in unison.

Marissa brushed off the mare's back, then smoothed the blanket out and picked up the saddle, throwing it over the mare's back. She reached under grabbing the cinch, lacing it through the buckle and pulled it tight. She kneed the mare in the side, then pulled again on the cinch and fastened it. She adjusted the stirrups at just the right length.

Shad stood watching this inexperienced young woman saddle a horse like she had been doing it all her life.

She turned when she was finished, her face beaming with a smile that seemed to light up the entire area. "I'm gonna name her Muffin." She said proudly.

"Horse don't need no name, but if that's what you want, let's git back to town." Shad said, turning back to the foreman. "Thanks, Rogers."

# CHAPTER THREE

"So long, Folks. You got yourself a fine animal, Miss. Y'all be careful. So long." He turned back to the corral.

Shad climbed aboard his horse and headed out with Marissa and Muffin right behind him.

"Thank you, Shad," she said, riding up beside him.

"For what?" he asked, looking straight ahead.

"For Muffin, I love her. Thank you so much."

"No need to thank me. You needed a horse. You got a horse. Simple and done with. Now, let's git back to town. It's gonna be too late to take off today, so first thing in the morning we'll be hitting the trail."

"I'll be ready," she said excitedly.

"Meet me at the café at six," he told her and kicked his horse in the sides leaving her behind.

Shad pulled up in front of the livery stable and dismounted.

"I figured you got a horse when Mildred came back. Where's Marissa?" he asked, looking down the road.

"She'll be along. Take care of my horse, I'm going to the general store. How you know Marissa's name?"

"I reckon everbody knows Marissa. She's got the sweetest voice I ever heard."

"Tell her where I went," he turned and walked away.

Shad had finished getting supplies when Marissa came through the door.

"Hello, Marissa," said Thaddeus Miller, the owner. "Be right with you."

"Thanks, Mr. Miller, I'm with this gentleman and I use that word very loosely, 'cause he don't seem to know the meaning of the word." She glared at Shad.

"What got your drawers in a bunch?" he asked surprised.

"Did you forget already that we're partners?" she was almost in tears.

"I ain't forgot. How could I forget, although I think I might like to. I ain't never had a partner, so you need to have a little patience and let me git used to the idea."

Marissa wiped at her nose and said, "I reckon I can understand this time, but don't leave me in the dust like you just done."

"Like I said, it's gonna take some gitting used to." He turned to Mr. Miller. "Sack all this stuff up and I'll . . . we'll be back for it in the morning."

"Yes sir. It'll be ready when you are."

"Come on, Partner. I'll buy you supper."

They walked down the street to Wentworth's Café. Shad opened the door, stepped to the side and motioned

Marissa to go in. She went ahead and he realized why he liked to go first. He didn't get to watch her swaying hips if he went first.

It seemed he wasn't the only one that noticed her. All the men in the place stopped eating and stared at her.

They sat at the only empty table in the place. When the waitress came over, they ordered the pork chop special.

They finished the rest of the meal without talking, which suited Shad. The less talking the better is the way he felt. He speared the last bite of meat and shoved it in his mouth, using the napkin, he wiped his mouth and pushed his chair back, telling Marissa, without saying anything that he was ready to go. She quickly ate the last of her meal, without enjoying it, wiped her mouth, pushed back her chair and stood.

"Well, she said, sounding a little angry. Let's go, we're burning daylight."

Shad looked up and at Marissa. She had surprised him, but he wasn't about to let her know it. "You go ahead; I'll settle the bill."

She nodded, placed her hat on her head, turned and headed for the door. Shad watched as she walked away. The swaying of her hips in those trousers caused a stirring inside that he thought he had shut off a long time ago. He chastised himself for having thoughts such as these. *'Maybe later,* he thought to himself. *Not yet, not now, not until I find the men I'm looking for and bring them to justice.'* He gave money to Lizzie, the owner's daughter. *'After all, we are almost kin. But we're not. Not really. We're in laws.'*

# CHAPTER FOUR

The next morning after another restless night Shad came down the stairs of the hotel and there was Marissa standing fussing with the desk clerk.

"I done told you a hundred times, I ain't interested. Why can't you get it through your thick skull that it ain't never gonna happen."

"Ah, come on Miss Marissa. If you'd only give me a chance. I think you might be surprised.

Shad stepped up to the couple and said, "Is this gent bothering you?" he looked directly at the clerk, his eyes seemed to be shooting flames.

"No, he ain't bothering me. You ready to go?"

"Sure, let's git our stuff at the store and git on the road."

In short time they were on the road heading east, the way Marissa said the outlaws headed.

They had been riding non-stop and it was getting close to dark. Shad had noticed Marissa was sitting high in the saddle.

"There's a place up ahead where we'll stop for the night. You ain't done much riding, have you?"

She didn't answer, but Shad saw a pained expression on her face. He guided his horse into a small clearing with plenty of trees and a small stream.

He reined up, dismounted, then turned to see Marissa practically falling from the saddle. She leaned her head against the side of Muffin. She slowly reached back with both hands and gently touched her back side. She jerked her hand back when it made contact.

Shad walked over to her and helped her over to a large tree. "You wanna try to sit?" he asked.

"I don't think I can," she answered. "I'm sorry, Shad, I didn't want to be any trouble for you."

"You ain't exactly trouble. I understand you ain't never rode a horse much. It could happen to anybody. We can stay here for a couple of days and give you time to heal up. We don't have to be in any hurry."

"That's real nice of you to do that for me."

"Wait here," he went to his saddlebags and pulled out a brown bottle, bringing it back.

"Liniment," he gestured to the bottle. Rub this own and in a couple days you'll be good as new."

"Thanks," she said, reaching for the bottle.

"Maybe you ortta let me rub in on for you."

"I think I can do it myself," she said, disappearing into the brush.

"Okay, but when you can't reach, let me know."

Shad was finishing making a pot of coffee when he heard, "Shad?"

"Yeah."

"I can't reach, could you help, please/"

"Sure," he said, closing the lid on the coffee pot. "You gonna come out here by the fire or you want me to come in there?"

"I just stick it out between the bushes and you can rub some on."

"Okay, but I think it would be better if you came out here."

She stepped through the bushes holding her pants with one hand and the bottle in the other.

"Drop'em and let me do this."

She pushed her trousers down.

Shad stood for a moment, gazing at her bottom, which should have been white in color, but was a blistering red. He poured a little liquid into his hand and rubbed gently. "Well," he said, "that answers that question."

"That feels good," she said. "That answers what question?"

"I was wondering if you and Melissa are identical in every way."

"She didn't have that little heart shaped birthmark, did she?"

"Nope, she didn't and I might say it's a very pretty birthmark too."

"How many more times do we have to rub on that liniment?" she asked as she pulled up her pants and brushed them off as she stood.

"A couple more times should do it. Maybe if we hadn't ridden so far in one sitting. Come on and git somethin' to eat. You want some coffee?"

"Yes, thank you and by the way, I have to complement you on your cooking." As she chewed a piece of bacon. "It was very good."

"Anybody can fry bacon and warm beans. Ain't no trick to that."

"I noticed something different about the coffee. Do you have a secret recipe for it?"

"I put just a tad of cinnamon in the pot. It gives it that special taste you're talking about."

"I'll have to remember that. It's very good."

Shad stood, went to the horses and retrieved the bed rolls, brought them back and started spreading them next to the fire. He put his on one side and Marissa's on the other.

"That sure looks inviting. I didn't realize until this minute how tired I am. Thank you for spreading my bed roll for me."

"I only did it 'cause you're feeling poorly. When you're better I'll expect you to pull your own weight."

"Sounds fair to me," she said. "Good night Shad."

"Goodnight." Shad lay awake for quite a while that night. He couldn't get the picture of Marissa's bare bottom out of his head. Finally, he fell into a restless sleep. The next morning came only too quickly. Marissa was still asleep, so he went about starting the fire and making something to eat.

Everything was almost ready when he heard her say, "Umm, that smells good. I could get used to this real easy."

"You remember what I told you last night. When you're better."

"I know; I'll have to do things myself. But right now, I would like some of that delicious coffee."

Shad poured a cup and handed it to her. He watched as she puckered her lips to blow on the hot liquid. When he realized what he was doing, he quickly averted his eyes and stirred the beans.

"Better grab a plate and eat while it's hot. I'm gonna go check on the horses."

He poured himself a cup of coffee and went to where the horses were tied.

*'I need to get my mind on business and keep those thoughts out of my mind.'* It was like he had no control over his mind or his eyes. It was like she was a magnet and kept drawing his eyes to look at her. *'She looks like Melissa, yet she doesn't. Maybe it's her mannerisms. She sure is something to look at. I have to admit that.'*

"Shad?"

"Yeah?"

"You think I could go for a swim in that stream?"

"I reckon if that's what you want to do. You don't have to ask my permission. You're a big girl and can make your own decisions."

"You could maybe find something else to do for a short time, couldn't you?"

"Sure, I could ride up the trail a little ways and kind of scout out the land. Maybe be gone 'bout half an hour."

"Thanks, Shadrack, I appreciate that so much."

"You just be done in half an hour 'cause I'm coming back. I don't think I'll see much more than you've already showed me."

"Go ahead and leave so I can get in that water."

"On my way." He tightened the cinch and mounted up. He tipped his hat to Marissa and rode out of camp.

He was on his way back when he heard a scream. He spurred his horse and rode into camp.

"Shadrack!" Marissa called loudly. "Help!"

He jumped off his horse and ran toward the stream. Marissa was in the middle of the water pointed toward the bank.

"What's wrong," he asked, looking at her standing there in the all-together.

"There's a snake on the bank."

"Where?" he searched the area. "I don't see any snake. It probably ran away when you started screaming."

"It was right there," she pointed at a small clump of bushes.

Shad moved closer and he saw it. It was a water moccasin about three feet long. He pulled his pistol and shot its head off. Marissa was still standing in the water. "It's okay to come out now."

She continued to stand as if frozen in time.

"Marissa!" Shad hollered.

All of a sudden, she snapped out of the trance she seemed to be in and realized she was standing in the water without any clothes on and Shad was standing on the bank watching her. "Shadrack, turn around!" she shouted.

"Why?" he asked. "I done seen everything you got. Come on out and get dressed." He turned and walked back to camp. He tossed a couple of sticks on the fire and pushed the coffee pot closer to the flame.

Shortly, Marissa came up fully clothed. "It seems I'm always having to say thank you, doesn't it?"

"Don't have to. I'd done the same thing for anybody."

"I'm still thankful to you. I'm deathly afraid of snakes."

"You had a right to be scared of that one. It was a water moccasin. One bite from it and you'd been dead in a short time."

"Just thinking about it causes me to shiver."

"I can tell you how to fix that."

"How?"

"Don't think about it."

"Oh you," she wrinkled up her face at him.

He liked this woman, he decided at that moment. *'Maybe it's time to start thinking about a relationship. But with Melissa's sister? Is that a good idea?'*

"What are you thinking so serious about?" she asked.

"To tell the truth, I was thinking about you."

"What about me?"

"I was wondering if you and I should get better acquainted."

"I thought you didn't want to get involved yet, not until you brought Melissa's killers to justice."

"I didn't, but that was before I met you."

"I'm not sure it's a good idea."

"Why not? We're both unattached."

"When I get serious about a man, I don't want any competition."

"I just told you I was unattached."

"Yes, you may be single, but you still have very strong feelings for Melissa."

"I'll never forget her, if that's what you're asking me to do."

"I'm not saying you have to forget her. I loved her too, but life goes on. Just move her to another place in your mind. I expect to be front and center when a man thinks about me that way."

"I don't know if I can do that, at least not right away."

"I can wait, just let me know when you think you can put me first."

"You'll be the first to know, now we better get some sleep. Morning's gonna come mighty early."

"Any more coffee?" she asked. "I think I need one after that scare."

"Sure, I think there's a couple cups left. Pour me one if you don't mind."

"Why would I mind?" she teased. "You're my hero."

"You got me mixed up with somebody else, 'cause I sure ain't no hero."

"You'll always be my hero," she said as she passed him a cup of coffee.

He took the cup and her hand brushed against his. He almost dropped the cup her skin touched his.

"What's the matter?" she asked. "You seem nervous."

"It's nothing," he said and drank part of the liquid, then tossed the rest on the ground. "I'm going to bed. Good night."

"Good night, Hero."

Shad was haven't a hard time controlling his heart beat. It seemed to want to burst out of his chest. He lay on his bedroll and turned his back to Marissa. Sleep was slow coming this night.

"Come on, Shad, get up," he felt somebody pushing on his shoulder. "Come on sleepy head, you gonna sleep away the day?"

"What time is it?" he asked sitting up. Looks to be almost noon."

"Yeah," she told him. "You had a mighty restless night so I let you sleep this morning. What was wrong with you last night?"

"Just some old memories and some new thoughts. We need to hit the trail if we're gonna find them hombres."

"There's some bacon and a little bit of hard-tack if you want it. Coffee makes it almost edible."

"You saddled the horses?" he looked around as he poured a cup of black coffee into a cup."

"Yeah, I figured you'd be raring to go once you woke up."

Shad pushed a couple pieces of bacon in his mouth, chewed a couple of times, then took a big swig of coffee to wash it down. He poured the remainder of the liquid on the fire and kicked dirt over the dying embers. He walked to his horse and stowed the cup in his saddle bag.

"Let's ride," he mounted, kicked his horse in the ribs and left at a gallop.

Marissa had to hurry to catch up and when she did, she said, "Did you forget you've got a partner now?"

"Sorry," he looked straight ahead.

Shad had a habit of riding into each town looking straight ahead. When Marissa questioned him about it, he said, "I figure it's gonna end either of two ways. I'll find them and kill them if they won't give up and it'll be over.

Or on the other side, I git killed where it'll be over. Either way, it's done and over with."

"You sound kind a fatalistic about that. Don't you want to live or don't you care?"

"Like I said, I just want this to be over with, one way or another."

"I hope you'll reconsider in the next town. I don't want to lose a partner just when I got one."

"Old habits die hard." He continued looking straight ahead.

# CHAPTER FIVE

They rode another few miles and spotted a town in the distance. Shad spurred his horse and took off, again leaving Marissa where she was.

"Shad," she started to call. "Oh, what's the use? Such a hard-headed man." She followed and reached the edge of town when she heard a rifle shot and watched as Shad was knocked from the saddle landing hard in the dirt.

She rode slowly down the street, scanning the rooftops for any movement. She spotted a man standing looking down from the roof of the hotel. He had a rifle in his hand pointed at Shad. Marissa drew her weapon and fired, watched as the man grasped his chest and tumbled from the roof, landing on top of the porch, then rolling to the ground. She didn't bother checking to see if he was alive. If her shot hadn't killed him, that fall would have.

She climbed off Muffin and ran to Shad's side. She knelt down and cradled his head in her lap. A crowd was beginning to gather to see what was going on. "Well, don't just stand there gawking, get a doctor!"

Shad opens his eyes and looks at Marissa, "Did you get him?"

"I got him. How you doing?"

"I believe I've been shot. My back feels kinda numb. I ain't never been shot before."

One of the men stepped from the crowd. "I'm the doctor. Let me take a look?"

He opened Shad's shirt and looked at the wound. "He might have a chance if I get that slug out pronto. Some of you men carry him to my office and be careful with him."

Some men picked Shad up and started down the street behind the doctor. The doctor turned, looked at Marissa and asked, "You coming?"

"As soon as I see to the horses," she replied. "I'll be right there, and Doc?"

"Yeah," he answered.

"He better not die before I get there, you hear me?" she gathered the reins of Shad's horse and walked back to Muffin, grabbed her reins and headed to the livery stable at the end of the street.

An old man wearing dirty overalls and a slouch hat was standing taking in all the excitement.

"Howdy, Missy. You with the feller that got shot?"

"Yes, why?" Marissa looked at him with a questioning look.

"That feller got shot." he started. "His name Meshack?"

"Could be, why you asking?"

"Well, there was some more men with that feller you shot off the roof and when they come to town. I overheard'em talking 'bout yer feller. Said they'd be waitin' at the Standish Mine over in the next county. Thought ye might could use that information, 'case yer man don't make it. I'll take ker of yer animals, you go ahead and see to yer man."

"Thank you, you're very kind," she nodded and rushed down the street in the direction the doctor went. She scanned all the building looking for a Doctor's sign. She spotted one about half way down the street.

She rushed through the door and watched as the doctor pushed a scissor looking thing into Shad's back, twisting it around, then pulling it out holding a .45 caliber lead slug.

He turned to place it in a bowl and saw Marissa.

"Another inch in either direction and he wouldn't have made it this long. And he's not completely out of the woods yet. He your man?"

"Yes," she replied, quickly. "He's my man."

"Good," he said. "He's gonna need some love to pull through this and maybe a prayer or two wouldn't hurt none either."

"I can take care of both those things," she said somberly. Thanks Doc."

"I've got to go see another patient for a little while. I want you to give him a half spoonful of this medicine if I'm not back in time. Think you can do that?"

"I can do that," she said. Anything else I can do?"

"If he gets a fever, you need to keep him warm. I've got to go. I'm running late as it is. I'll be back as soon as I can." He picked up his bag and went out the door.

"Well, Shadrack," Marissa said. "You done it. You got yourself shot and you might not make it. But, I ain't gonna let you leave this world without a fight on my part. You're gonna have to fight too. You hear me?"

She gave him half a spoonful of medicine like the Doc said to do, then covered him with more blankets when he started shivering.

Shad was mumbling something, but Marissa couldn't understand it.

"I'm here, Shadrack, "she told him over and over. I ain't gonna leave you. And Shad, when you get better, I think we need to talk about that relationship you was talking about. I think I might like that."

"Marissa, that you?" he asked, opening his eyes and then closing them again.

"It's me," she told him. "I'm right here and I ain't going no place."

Shad kept tossing and turning, kicking the blankets off and she had to keep putting them back on him.

The doctor came back and looked at Shad. "I do believe he's going to make it, but don't get your hopes too high. He's not completely out of the woods yet. He's going to need a lot of bed rest."

"Is it alright if I stay here with him?" she asked.

"Sure, I reckon that would be the best for him. I wouldn't want him to wake and not see a familiar face."

"Thanks Doc, I appreciate that. He's kinda special to me."

"Well, I got to go out again. Some days it don't let up at all. I'll be back when I can. You keep him warm and give him as much water as he'll take."

Shad regained consciousness after three days. Three long days for Marissa as she didn't sleep much, just a cat nap when she could.

On that third day, Shad sat up in bed as if nothing was wrong with him. He looked at Marissa who was dozing in the chair beside the bed.

"Where am I?' he asked, Marissa didn't hear him, so he said it a little louder. "Where am I!"

Marissa jerked upright and almost fell off the chair. "You're awake."

"Course, I'm awake," he growled. "Where am I? Where's my clothes?

"You're in the doctor's office," she explained. "You got shot. Don't you remember?"

"All I know is we need to get outta here and go after them hombres. Now where's my clothes?" he swung his legs over the side of the bed. "And my boots. Where's my boots?"

"Shadrack, you ain't fit to go no place," she argued, "The doctor said it'd be another four or five days before you'll be healed enough to get outta bed. Now lay back down, please."

"You gonna git me my clothes or not?" he started to stand, wobbled a little, then straightened.

The doctor came in the room and said loudly, "What do you think you're doing?"

"I appreciate ever thing you done, but I gotta git outta here."

The doctor couldn't talk Shad out of leaving. Marissa finally gave in and helped him dress.

"I bought you a new shirt. The doctor had to cut the other one off. Are you sure you're up to this?"

"Let's go," he said, as he buckled his gun belt around his waist.

"Thanks Doc," Marissa handed him ten dollars.

"He really needs more bed rest," the doctor said, shaking his head. "There's no guarantee he'll survive so soon out of bed."

"Thanks again," Marissa said, as she followed Shad out the door.

They walked up the street to the livery stable where the old timer said, "Good to see you made it, Mr. Meshack. Word around town was laying bets against you gitting well. I made me a couple of dollars 'cause I bet you would."

"Would you quit yammering and git my horse," Shad fussed at the man.

"Done got'em, when I saw ye coming outta the Doc's office. Where 'bouts y'all headed."

"You're old enough to know better than to ask that question, but since you been so good to our animals, I'm gonna tell you. We're headed out to catch the hombres that killed my family."

"Shore hope you catch'em. So long."

Shad climbed into the saddle a little slow, but once there he looked determined to do this job.

Marissa handed the hostler five dollars, shook his hand, slipped her foot in Muffin's stirrup and pulled herself into the saddle, turned the animal, and headed in the direction Shad had gone. Thankfully he wasn't riding too fast, so she caught up rather quickly.

## CHAPTER SIX

They had ridden for about four hours and it didn't look as Shad was ready to stop any time soon. Marissa had turned in the saddle to check their back trail. When she turned back, she watched as Shad slowly slid from the saddle, landing hard onto the dirt road. She jumped from Muffin and rushed to his side. Kneeling down, she felt his forehead as she cradled his head in her lap. He was burning up with fever.

"Shadrack, you're gonna be the death of both of us." She glanced in both directions and spotted a small grove of trees about a hundred yards further on down the road, but how was she going to get Shad there? She laid his head down and walked to her horse. She removed her bedroll, carrying it back to where Shad was laying. She unrolled it, spreading it out next to his unconscious body. She rolled him onto the bedroll, then retrieved a rope from the saddle and secured it to the bedroll. She tied the other end to the saddle horn. She took Muffin's reins and slowly led her toward the trees. The horse balked a little because she wasn't used to pulling something like this. When they reached the area, she halted Muffin, gave her a pat on the neck, telling what a good horse she was. She untied the rope and tried pulling the bedroll, but she could only get it to budge a little.

"Now what?" She tied the rope back on the saddle horn. Talking calming to Muffin she led her into the trees, stopping beside the largest one. Again, she complemented her horse and untied the rope. As soon as she had Shad covered with the other bed roll, she brought Shad's horse under the trees. She removed both saddles and hobbled them next to the smaller trees.

Shad was laying on his bedroll. Marissa was removing a bottle of whisky from the saddlebags when the whole area lit up bright. Marissa turned to see a beam of light slide out of the heavens and settle on Shads unconscious body. His body seemed to quiver and shake lifting almost off the pallet, then settled back down. The beam of light ascended back into the clouds. Marissa stood as if frozen to the spot until she heard Shad moan. She rushed to his side and knelt beside him.

"Where am I," he mumbled.

"You're alright," Marissa said.

He sat up, looking around, "How come we stopped?" he asked.

"Don't you remember?" she replied. "You had a fever and we had to stop. Don't you remember anything?"

"I remember getting shot in that town. You say we was traveling?"

"Yes. You got better and decided we needed to get on the trail, Against the doctor's orders and my advice."

"How long we been here?"

"Almost a day and a half. I thought you was gonna die. Did you feel it?"

"Feel what? What're you talking about?"

"Feel that light. It came right out of the clouds and went into your body. I figure that's what saved you."

"I didn't feel nothing, but I ain't surprised it happened. Ain't the first time something like that has happened."

"What do you mean, not the first time?"

"When I was in that burning cabin, where Melissa and our unborn baby died. Something like this happened. Everybody said I should have died that night. Nobody could explain how I got out of that burning inferno, but there I was with very few burns. The preacher claimed God's hand was on me, but the way I figure is God let me live so's I could hunt down the scum that did it and bring them to justice."

"Well, I don't understand what happened, but I'm so very grateful. I don't want to lose you, Shadrack."

"I ain't going no place. Now, is there any coffee in that pot over yonder? I got a hankering for some hot coffee."

"I'll get you some, you just rest easy." She poured a cup for him and one for herself. She carried it back and handed it to him. She knelt on her knees next to him and lifted the cup to her lips blowing on the hot liquid before sipping it slowly.

Shad followed suit, blowing on his cup, then sipping. "Umm. That is good," he said.

"Sure is, I put that cinnamon in it like you said and it's a lot better when you got somebody to share it with."

"I just remembered something," Shad said, looking across the fire at her.

"Yeah, what do you remember?"

"I remember you saying you would like to start a relationship with me."

"How can you remember something that never happened?"

"You telling me you didn't say it?

"Well, I might have said it, but only to get you to wake up when you were unconscious."

"So, you did say it?"

"I reckon I did, but it was like I said. To get you to wake up."

"Well, I'm awake now. What have you got to say now?"

"Maybe I meant it, but then again, maybe I didn't."

"You got to go one way or the other. I think you know how I feel."

"Yeah, but remember what I said about being second in your mind."

"I believe I can put you first. At least I'll try very hard."

"Why don't we continue the way we are, for now. Maybe when this is over, we can think about a relationship. How's that sound?"

"Well, I can't force you to care for me, so I reckon that's what we'll do."

"I didn't say I didn't care for you. I do. Very much, it's just we got this job to do, then we can get on with our lives."

"Okay, then let's go git these culprits so we can get on with our lives, together."

"You sure you're ready?  After all, you just got up from a bad fever."

"I feel great, sorta refreshed if you know what I mean. If you're ready, I'm ready."

"Let me clean and pack up these utensils and I'll be ready," she started picking up everything.

"I'll git the horses ready," he said, standing slowly and looking a little washed out in the face, but he straightened up and continued on.

He had just thrown the saddle across the back of Muffin when a shot ricocheted off the big tree where the horses were tethered.

Shad hit the ground, rolling behind the tree, pulling his pistol and shouted to Marissa to take cover. He peeked around the tree and another shot sent splinters into his gun hand, causing him to drop the weapon and jerk his hand back.

"You okay, Shad?" Marissa shouted.

"I'm okay, you?"

"I'm okay, but I don't have my guns," she shouted back. "You sure you're alright? I saw you drop your pistol."

"Just a few splinters. If I can reach around and grab my gun, we'll get out of this mess in no time."

He slipped his hand around the tree and a slug scattered dirt in the air. He jerked back and tried to calm his breathing.

*"Come on Shadrack,"* he thought to himself. *"This ain't the first trouble you been in. Slow down and concentrate. There's always a way."* He began to relax and felt a peacefulness come over him and he stood up, leaned against the tree and stepped out from its cover. Dirt was being tossed into the air as bullets began to hit the ground all around him.

"Shad," Marissa hollered. "What are you doing? Get down."

Shad kept walking toward the shooter. Somehow, the slugs weren't hitting him as he got closer and closer.

The man doing the shooting stepped from behind his cover, sighted down the barrel and slowly squeezed the trigger. Nothing happened. The rifle didn't fire. The man looked at it, then throwing it to the ground, he reached for his pistol. By this time Shad was upon him, reached and clamped his hand on the man's hand just as his pistol was sliding from the holster.

Shad squeezed and twisted causing the man to drop to his knees. Shad released his hand and stepped back as the man grabbed his crushed hand with his other.

"What kind of man are you?" the man cursed Shad. "I ain't never seen nobody like you before. I put those bullets right between your eyes and nary a one hit you."

"I'm just a man who wants justice and you're lucky that's what I want, otherwise you'd be dead. Now you gonna tell me where your buddies are?"

"I don't know what you're talking about. I ain't got no buddies."

"It'd be a lot easier for you if you quit lying."

"I ain't lying. I'm alone."

"How come you shot at us, if you're by yourself?"

"A couple fellers offered me a hundred dollars if I got rid of you. Do you know how long it'd take me to earn a hundred dollars?"

"Did you ever think you might not live to spend that hundred?"

"Why wouldn't I?"

"I could kill you right now, right here. Think on that a spell."

"Whatcha gonna do with me?"

"Ain't decided. You sit there and ponder what you want to do with the rest of your life if I don't shoot you."

Shad walked back to the tree where Marissa was standing. "You okay?" he asked her.

"Yeah, it's just a scratch," and she slumped to the ground.

Shad glanced back at the man on the ground, "You move and you're a dead man." He knelt beside Marissa. "Where you hit?" he asked.

She didn't answer. She had lost consciousness. He bent over her and saw the slug had entered just to the left of her shoulder. He rolled her over and saw that it had went all the way through, but now he had to stop the bleeding. He pulled her bandana from around her neck and pressed it hard against the wound. He did the same with his bandana on her back. He turned to the man sitting on the ground. "You got a knife?"

"Yeah, I got a knife. Why?"

"Stick the blade in the fire to sterilize it, then come over here and cauterize this bullet hole you made."

"I can't be putting my knife in the fire, it'll ruin it."

"If you don't, you ain't gonna have no use for a knife. Now do what I said and be quick about it."

The man stood, pulled his knife from his pants unfolded the blade and stuck it in the flames. It didn't take long for it to be glowing red.

"Alright, bring it over and do this. Better use something so's you don't burn your hand."

The man used his handkerchief and brought the hot knife over. "What do I do?" he asked, hesitating.

"Press the blade against the wound, pull it off and press it on the back when I roll her over."

The man pressed the blade against the wound and then the same to her back.

"Okay, now you go sit back down and maybe I'll consider letting you go."

"I'm shore sorry 'bout your girlfriend. I didn't really want to shoot you, but it sounded like easy money. If you let me go, I'll tell them fellers I shot you and you're dead. That ortta be worth something to you."

"You just sit for a spell." Shad leaned close to Marissa's face and said, "Looks like we got something else in common. This kinda makes us even closer, don't you think?"

Her face was pale and she was beginning to shiver. "Bring a blanket over here," he shouted to the man. "And be quick about it."

The man brought a blanket over and handed it to Shad. "She gonna be okay?" he asked.

"She better be, 'cause your life depends on it. "

" I didn't mean to shoot her," he said in a pleading voice.

"That don't make no never mind now. You did."

"Why don't you just let me ride outta here? You won't never see me again."

"Why don't you go over yonder and set yourself down outta the way. I'll deal with you later."

Shad wrapped the blanket around Marissa and cradled her in his arms. "You got to get better. We got some unfinished business, you and me. I don't think we ortta wait to catch them bandits afore we get better acquainted. I reckon I done fell in love with you. Head over heels in love."

Marissa moaned and opened her eyes. "Did I just hear you say you loved me?"

"You sure did. How you feeling? Now that's a dumb question. I reckon I ortta know how it feels to get shot. You jest rest easy. I'll get some broth made and you'll be up and around in no time."

"Shad?"

"Yeah, Sugar."

"I don't want no broth. I want a steak. I'm awful hungry."

"I don't think I can git you a steak out here where we are, but I kin send our guest to town to bring one back. Would that be alright?"

"I guess it'll have to be if I want a steak."

"You rest and I'll git this hombre on the road." He stood and walked over to the man. "Did you hear that?"

"Yeah, I heard. You want me to go to town and get her a steak. What makes you think I'll come back once I'm outta sight?"

"I reckon you know the answer to that, now don't you?"

"Okay, I'm going, but I'm gonna expect something in return."

"We'll talk about that when you get back. Now I suggest you get on the road and hurry."

"I got a problem."

"What's your problem?"

"I ain't got no money. That's how come I took this job in the first place."

Shad gave him a twenty-dollar gold piece. "I'm expecting you to be back in a couple hours. You know what will happen if you don't come back, don't you?"

"What if I run into the hombres that wants you dead? They might like it that I didn't get the job done."

"You tell'em if they want me dead to come do that little job themselves. And tell'em they'd better let you come back here. Now move out."

## CHAPTER SEVEN

Spurring his horse, he left in a cloud of dust.

Shad walked back to Marissa and was surprised to see her sitting up leaning against the tree.

"Well, you're doing okay. You want some coffee? Got a fresh pot brewing."

"That sounds good. Add a couple spoons of sugar, would you?"

"I thought you liked your coffee black."

"Just got a hankering for something sweet. You don't mind, do you?"

"Anything you want. That's what I'm gonna do. Be right back with sweet coffee."

Shad walked back to the fire and poured a cup full of coffee, adding two heaping spoons of sugar. He stirred it, grabbed a biscuit, then carried it back to Marissa.

"Here you go, "He handed her the biscuit." then he set the cup on the ground beside her.

"Umm. This is really good. Where's the coffee?"

"Right here." he reached down, picked it up and handed to her. He grabbed it as she almost dropped it.

"Maybe I'm not as good as I thought," she said, looking up at him.

"That's okay, I got this. I'll hold it for you. Just take little sips. There you go, that's the way."

She took one last swallow, then pushed the cup away. "That's enough for now. Thank you."

"Ain't nothing to thank me for. You'd done the same for me, in fact you did the same for me already."

"What are you going to do with the man that shot me? I think you should let him go, that is after he comes back with my steak."

"Let's talk about it when he gets back. Right now the best thing for you is to rest. Lay back down, close your eyes and relax."

She scooted down onto the pallet. Shad pulled the blanket up around her neck and noticed she was already asleep. He picked up her cup, stood and walked back to the fire.

*'I'm gonna have to do something about them scoundrels. I ain't gonna let'em take Marissa the way they took Melissa.'*

He touched the handle of his. 45, perhaps from habit or perhaps for reassurance. Releasing the handle, he pulled a bandana out of his pocket and wiped his face. As he sat on an old log beside the fire, he watched as Marissa's chest moved up and down with her breathing. Shaking his head while thinking, "I'm gonna ask her to marry me, tomorrow."

He was sitting by the fire watching Marissa when a shot rang out, splintering the log which he was sitting on. He fell over the back of it, pulling his weapon as he fell. Another shot whizzed past his head when he tried to look over this hiding place.

"Who are ya and what do you want?" he hollered, all the time knowing who it was.

"I don't reckon we need no introduction, now do we?" a gruff voice responded. "I see your gal is laid up over by the tree. I'll give you until the count of three to throw out your gun, and come on out or I'm gonna put a bullet in her. One, two, thr . . ."

"Hold on, I'm coming out," Shad hollered, then tossed his .45 out. He stood slowly, then stepped over the log next to the fire.

"Well, well, you're in luck," said the gruff voice. "The boss wants you alive, so's he can have some fun watching you squirm. Now, walk over here and we'll take us a little ride. You last ride, Ha! Ha!"

Shad said calmly, "I ain't going no place with you. I got to stay with her," he nodded toward Marissa.

"I can take care of that little problem," he pointed his pistol in Marissa's direction.

"Alright," Shad relented. "I get your point. I'll go with you, but can I at least tell her goodbye?"

"Wouldn't be very Christian like, if I didn't let you at least do that, now would it? Go ahead, but make it quick."

"Thanks," he walked over to Marissa and knelt down beside her.

"My gun's in my holster," she whispered. "Can you reach it?"

Shad bent down as if he was going to kiss her, slipped her gun from its holster and into his vest. "So long, Darling," he said, standing, turning toward the two men.

"Wasn't that sweet," said the gruff voice. "You ready now?"

Shad walked to his horse, bent down as if he was going to tighten the cinch, pulled his pistol and fired, then fell to the ground rolling to his left and firing again. The result was two men lying face up in the dirt.

He stood, ejected the two spent cartridges and replaced them., walked over to the men and kicked their guns away, then he walked back to Marissa.

"You got'em. Did you get hit?" she sounded worried.

"Nope, I reckon I lucked out again. I'm just glad you was awake enough to tell me about your pistol."

"Shad?" Marissa said quietly.

"Yeah," he answered squatting down by her.

"Could you, I mean would you . . .," she hesitated.

"Sure, I reckon I can do that," he bent down and pressed his lips to hers.

"Uhh!" one of the men groaned loudly. "Help me," he groaned again.

Shad stood and walked over to the man. "I don't figure there's anybody can help you now. That's a bullet in your belly. You know what that means, don't you?"

"It means I'm gonna die and there ain't a blasted thang I can do about it."

"No, you can't do nothing about it. You shoulda thought of that before you come looking for me. There is something that might make it easier on you."

"What's that?" he moaned the words.

"You could go out with a clear conscious. Tell me the name and whereabouts of your boss."

"I can't do that." He said, coughing bubbles of blood coming out of his mouth.

"Why not? He can't do nothing to you now. Might help your entrance into eternity. Tell me before it's too late."

"Alright, his name is . . ., he started coughing and spitting more blood. "Carmelo Martinez," he moaned again, and tried to finish speaking, but it was no use, those were his last words.

"Thanks pardner," Shad said, He stood, bent down, grabbed the man's feet and dragged him into the bushes away from camp, then did the same with the other.

He walked back to Marissa. "He tell you anything?" she asked.

"Yeah, the boss is Carmelo Martinez. Didn't have time to say where he is though."

"I remember something the livery man said when you got shot," she said, then hesitated. "Uh. Something about . . .a Mine. Yeah, the Standish Mine. That's where they were supposed to meet up."

"And you're just now telling me." He was a little put out.

"I just now remembered. We have been pretty business with other things," she shot right back. "Is there any fresh coffee?"

"You feeling better, are you?" he asked.

"I'd feel better if I had some coffee with a lot of sugar in it."

"How come you're all of a sudden wanting sugar in your coffee?" he asked. "You've always had it black."

"I can't explain it," she said. "I just have this hankering for something sweet."

"I'll git you a cup, don't go no place."

"That ain't funny," she said loudly.

"Depends where you're at, now don't it?"

He poured a cup of the black liquid, spooned in a couple of heaping spoons of sugar and carried it to Marissa.

"Here you go. It's hot," as he handed it to her. He watched as she took it in her tiny hand, watched as she puckered her lips, blew on it, then put it to her lips and sipped. He wondered what those lips would feel like with a real kiss.

"Shad?" she said his name so softly, he had to strain to hear.

"Yeah?" he said.

"Would you lay with me tonight? That is if you want to."

"I think you know I want to, but I figure you orta get better before we, well you know."

"I'm not asking for that," she explained. "I just need someone to hold me, please."

"Sure, I reckon I kin do that. I'll git my bedroll. Yours ain't big enough for both of us." He walked to the fire, picked up his pallet, carried it back and unrolled it next to Marissa.

"Hurry," she said. "I'm getting tired and I don't want to sleep until I know you're next to me."

He removed his gun belt and boots, then lay beside her. She reached and pulled him close. He could feel her breath on his throat as he put his arms around her. Soon, her breathing leveled out and there was a light snoring sound.

Shad lay there with Marissa in his arms and it felt as if she belonged there. He twisted onto his back and she cradled her head on his shoulder. He watched the twinkling stars until his eyelids became so heavy, he finally gave up and closed his eyes.

# CHAPTER EIGHT

The next morning came much too quickly. The bright yellow sun was almost too much for his sleepy eyes as he squinted. Rolling out of bed, he noticed Marissa was still sleeping. He went into the bushes, returning shortly. He stirred the coals, added some twigs and grass, fanned and blew on it until a flame appeared, then he tossed a couple sticks of wood to it. The flames caught and soon the fire was blazing.

He poured the remaining coffee on the ground, filled the pot with fresh water, dumped in some coffee grounds, added a pinch of cinnamon and pushed it close to the flame. He sliced a few pieces of bacon, placing them in the skillet. As soon as they were brown on one side, he flipped them over, then opened a can of beans and dumped it with the bacon.

"That sure smells good," he heard Marissa. "Shad, could you come here a minute?"

He pulled the skillet back from the flames and walked over. "What's wrong?" he asked.

"I need help getting up," she explained. "I need to go in the bushes."

"Grab my hand," he put his hand out, which she grabbed and she was able to stand. She was a bit wobbly, but soon straightened out enough to take off to the bushes.

Shad went back to the fire when he heard her holler. "Shad!" Shad!"

He dropped the spoon he was stirring with and rushed to the bushes. "What's wrong?" he asked. "You hurt?"

"I can't get my pants up, could you help me, please?"

He pushed the brush aside and there she was, standing with her pants about halfway up. He walked over and helped pull them up, then fastened the buttons. "Come on, let's get you back to bed."

He helped her walk back to the tree, when she said, "I don't want to lay anymore. You think I could sit by the fire?"

"Sure, if you think you're up to it."

"Won't know 'til I try," Shad helped her to the log on the other side of the fire.

"Looks like our breakfast is ruined," he said as he helped her to sit.

"I think all I want is coffee anyway, with . . ."

"I know, extra sugar. Coming right up."

Marissa continued to get better each day and three days after she was injured, she declared she was ready to ride.

"If you're sure you're up to it, I would like to get this done," Shad said, concerned about her.

"I told you I was okay," She fussed. "Now, let's go find this Martinez fellow."

While Shad saddled the horses, Marissa started packing up the utensils. Although she was going very slow.

Shad finished saddling the horses and noticed Marissa was moving slow, so he helped by rolling the bedrolls and tying them behind the saddles.

"You're moving mighty slow, you sure about this?" he asked.

"I do admit I'm not quite 100%, but I figure the more I move around, the quicker I'll get better," she answered, stuffing the items in a saddlebag. "There, all done," she said as she looked around the camp. "This has been an experience, ain't it? Finishing off a couple of bandits, then me getting shot and best of all you told me you love me and want to marry me. I'd say all in all, it's been quite an experience, don't you agree?"

"I reckon it has," he commented. "You need help gitting in the saddle?"

"No," she said, and reached for the saddle horn. "Oh," she moaned.

"Let me help you," Shad said, rushing to her side.

"I can do it," she said, emphatically. "It just hurts a little, but I can do it." She placed her boot in the stirrup, pulled herself in the saddle and proclaimed, "Told you I could do it," however, her face was white as a sheet from the exertion it had taken for her to accomplish the feat.

Shad, from his horse commented, "You hang on tight to your saddle horn. I don't want you falling off."

"I'm okay, let's ride," with that she took off, bouncing on her horse.

Shad was worried, so he hurried to catch up to her, where he rode close in case she did start to take a tumble.

They rode for almost two hours when Marissa pulled up on Muffin's reins. She grabbed her canteen, twisted off the top and raised it to her lips. When she tilted her head back to drink, her body continued to fall backward. Thankfully, Shad was close enough to catch her.

"Hold on there, girl. It's a long ways to the ground. You wanna stop for a while?" he asked.

Straightening up, she said, "I'm alright, just got a little light headed," she lifted the canteen again and took a long swallow. Wiping her mouth with her sleeve, she twisted the lid back on the canteen and hung it around the saddle horn. Without saying anything, she clicked to Muffin and took off again.

Shad shook his head and muttered, "Women." He gave his horse the go ahead and followed after her.

# CHAPTER NINE

A couple hours later, Shad pulled up on the reins and pointed, "The Standish Mine is just over that rise. Why don't you wait here and I'll check it out?"

"I've got a better idea," she told him. "Why don't you circle around and come in from the other end? I'll wait fifteen minutes and go in from this end. That way we got him from both directions. Something he won't be expecting."

"You be careful," he looked at her for a minute. "I've got plans for us later."

"I'll be careful," she smiled. "I've got a couple of ideas myself. Now let's do this done."

Shad rode off into the bushes and headed toward the other end of the Mine. It didn't take as long as he figured. "Should I go on in or wait the full fifteen minutes?" he asked himself. He decided to ride in alone, thinking he would keep Marissa out of it if there was a fight.

He was almost to the Mine office when a shot rang out and he heard the bullet whiz past his ear. He dropped from the saddle as if he had been hit hoping Martinez would think so and reveal where he was hiding.

Sure enough, when Shad glanced up, he saw the man open the door of the office and step out. He had just stepped down from the small porch when Marissa rode in from the other side.

Martinez whipped around and let go with a hasty shot that barely missed her. Shad jumped to his feet, drew his weapon and pulled the trigger three times, each slug, jerking him, each time a bullet entered his body. When he stopped his dance, he slumped to the ground, his body twitched one last time and then lay still.

Shad replaced the three cartridges and pushed his .45 back into the holster, picked up his hat, place it on his head, then glanced up at Marissa. She was sitting on Muffin with a stunned look on her face, then as if she realized she was alright, she climbed off Muffin and started running toward Shad. He started walking toward her. They met and Marissa threw her arms around his neck sobbing, "Why didn't you wait for me? Why won't you let me help? You could have been killed." She released him and stood back.

"I'm alright," he told her, as he reached and pulled her back against his body. "What do you say, let's get outta here?

**Books by J.C. Hulsey**

Angel Falls, Texas

Velvet Sky, Arizona

Angry Orchard, Colorado

Clear Stone, Wyoming

Itching Tree, Idaho

Windy Butte, New Mexico

Devil's Dance, Dakota Territory

Redemption Road

Red Rose

Rebecca

The Concho Kid

Ugly Mugly

GUTSHOT

The Last Ride

The Old Man

The Pistol Preacher

Shortland

Dynamite

The Concho Kid

Dead Man's Gun

Does Nora Know

Doke Walker

Brothers

Satan's Refuge

Shadrack

The Brute

The Decision

The Greenhorn

The Gunfight

The Hangman

The Old Timer

Trudy

The Waterhole

Welcome to Texas Hell

Some Stuff I Wrote

Some More Stuff I Wrote

Even More Stuff I Wrote

Newest Stuff I Wrote

Brand New Stuff I Wrote

Brand Spanking New Stuff I Wrote

Look What I Found

Oldest Coon Hunter in Somervell Co

(Compiled by)

Confessions of a Battered Wife

(Compiled by)